Billionaire Daddy Series

Lawyer Billionaire Daddy (Book 2)

S.E. Riley

The Redherring Publishing House

Lawyer Billionaire Daddy (Book 2)

Table of Contents

Prologue...1

Chapter 1 6

Chapter 2...13

Chapter 3...18

Chapter 4...26

Chapter 5...31

Chapter 6 36

Chapter 7...46

Chapter 8 53

Chapter 9 60

Epilogue...65

Prologue

Sophia Anderson stepped into the stuffy meeting room with a spring in her step. This would be her first real case since passing the bar. Finally, she had achieved her childhood dream, and she was part of an incredible team, alongside junior partner, Maria Martinez, her idol. She had previously worked with Maria as a paralegal and admired the woman greatly. To be invited to work with her as an associate on this case was a dream come true.

Sophia took her place at the table with a smile, leaning over to greet Maria. The older woman smiled back and nodded to her. The door on the opposite side of the room opened, and she settled into her seat, trying not to squirm like an excited schoolgirl. She knew this wouldn't be nearly as exciting in a week or two, but she'd loved her work as a paralegal and expected to love this too.

Her gaze lifted to the people entering from the other side of the meeting room. This would be the other team, the people they would have to beat if they wanted to get their client acquitted. When Sophia saw a familiar tall frame with piercing brown eyes and neatly combed dirty blond hair, she tensed and tried to stifle a gasp. Her breath hitched, strangling in her throat.

His gaze fell on her, and she spotted the tightening of his jaw. It was probably imperceptible to anyone else, but she knew it well. He was surprised too. He was better at hiding it than she was, though, and he moved to the head of the table across from

Maria without missing a step.

Maria leaned over with a tight smile. "Try not to be intimidated, Soph. His bark is worse than his bite."

Sophia forced a laugh. His bark was certainly *not* worse than his bite. Elijah Clarkson was not a man to be trifled with and was a good lawyer. Well, spectacular, actually, given his quick rise to senior partner at his firm. Why hadn't she realized a high profile case like this might draw him in? She was so screwed. Seeing him now brought the old feelings she'd held for him into sharp focus once again, and she shifted in her seat, avoiding his gaze. "I'm sure it is."

"I'd know," Maria murmured. "I dated the hard-nosed pain in the—"

Elijah's gaze was firmly on Sophia, weighing her down in the chair until she wanted to sink into it and hide. Whatever Maria was telling her in quiet murmurs was lost in the gravity of that look, and she couldn't help looking back. This was so bad.

Back in the day, since she was 8 and him 16, she and Elijah could argue until kingdom come, and the few times he'd been by to visit since his graduation from high school had proven their debates hadn't changed much. She didn't fear that she wouldn't be able to counter his arguments before the jury and judge.

Now, at 24, she feared her professionalism would be wrecked, losing her place in this case because of their past. She had to keep a lid on her attraction to him, that had been growing since she turned 16, and avoid letting on about their personal connection. Thankfully, Maria had no idea they'd known each other as children.

The meeting started, and Sophia tried to focus on taking notes as usual, but with Elijah's gaze boring a hole in the top of her bent head, she found it increasingly difficult to focus. The minutes ticked by in slow torture, and she was acutely aware of the clock's ticking behind the low murmur of the voices in the room as requests for information were handed over, and other official business was dealt with.

Finally, Elijah stood. She straightened in her seat, unsure why she felt the need to snap to attention when he did so. His movement signaled the meeting's end.

"Any further requests may be sent directly to me or my paralegal," he informed the room in his warm, low voice.

She suppressed a shiver and doodled on her notepad to distract herself.

"Sophia, may I speak to you in the hall?"

She looked up to find him standing next to her chair and stiffened, glancing at Maria for help.

"Why do you need to talk to my associate, Elijah?" Maria's voice held suspicion but remained professional in tone.

"She assisted as my paralegal a few times while going through law school. I haven't had a chance to congratulate her on passing the bar exam," he replied smoothly, waving his own gawking team out of the room. "I'll catch up," he told them.

"You can't congratulate her in here?"

"I had a small gift for her, and I see no reason why I need to explain myself to you, Maria. If Sophia has no objections, you shouldn't either. It's hardly unacceptable practice to give a newly minted lawyer hearty congratulations, regardless of which team she's playing for." His gaze returned to her. "Sophia? May I give you the gift privately? I didn't think you'd wish me to embarrass you in front of the entire team. Unless you've changed your opinion of making a display of gifts and congratulations for your work?"

She flushed and pushed away from the table. A bark worse than his bite, indeed! She had tremendous respect for Maria, but the woman clearly hadn't come to know Elijah like she did. If Sophia didn't cooperate, he'd give the gift—if there was one—here and leave her to squirm as he heaped on the praise in front of her team. "No, I haven't. We can speak in the hall."

"Soph," Maria warned.

"I won't take the gift in front of everyone in the court building, Maria. Don't worry. I know better than to make it look like I'm compromised or colluding with the other team."

Her boss nodded and sat back in her seat, seeming satisfied. "I'll see you back in the office."

She followed Elijah out into the hall with trepidation. When they had found a relatively private alcove by the windows on the left side of the building, she stopped and crossed her arms. "Well? Are you trying to make me look bad in front of Maria? I've worked too hard for this to let you screw it up for me, Elijah."

He smiled gently. "I have no intention of screwing it up for you, Soph. I really did want to congratulate you." He pulled a small box from his pocket and handed it to her. "I'd intended to stop by your floor in the building after the meeting to give it to you. I didn't know you'd be here today, but no sense in waiting. Open it later. I need to speak to you about the trial now while we have a moment."

She tucked it into her purse and waited with a raised brow. "Out with it, then, Elijah Clarkson."

He grinned. "My station and rank mean nothing to you, do they?"

"Not in private," she said. "Well?"

"Can you really handle working against me on this case?"

Though his question hit hard at her private doubts and fears, she rolled her eyes. "Have I ever had a problem arguing with you?"

"No, but that's not my concern, and you know it."

She looked away. No, it wasn't his concern, and it wasn't hers, either. Both of them knew the real question was whether she'd be able to remain professional and distant without falling into the usual patterns of their debates where they'd amicably make up and return to their usual close friendship. Seeing him as someone other than a friend had been difficult enough when she worked with him. Now she had to work against him, and she couldn't allow any indication they were friends to slip if she didn't want to risk accusations of misconduct and collusion.

"I can handle it, Elijah. Worry about yourself. I'm not the only one with habits of familiarity. What you just did in there...don't do it again if you intend to keep us both on the trial."

He tucked his hands into his pockets with a nod. "Very well. Soph?"

She lifted her gaze back to his.

"I meant what I said. Congratulations on passing the bar. I always knew you would."

She laughed, some of the tension between them easing to give way to their familiar warmth. "I have a habit of getting what I want."

"As do I." He grinned. "I suspect it's what makes us so good at butting heads."

"I suspect so. I suppose I'll see you at the next meeting or during depositions." She pushed past him, trying not to notice the warm cinnamon and spice of his cologne, and hurried down the hall toward the exit. Whatever happened in that courtroom, she had to maintain her distance. If she couldn't, they were both going to be in trouble.

Chapter 1

Two years later

Elijah stepped into the courtroom with a weary sigh. This trial had dragged on for two years, and he was more than ready for litigation to end. This was why clients usually tried to resolve disputes about breach-of-contract before they ever landed in court. Unfortunately, these two hadn't been able to resolve the differences, and his client's opponent had refused arbitration. So, here they were. Two long years of courtrooms and meetings to try to resolve the problems. Two long years of working against Sophia when he'd come to want nothing more than to have her on his side again.

Speaking of Sophia...

He eyed the brunette as she strode in and settled next to his ex, Maria. Sophia had been burning the midnight oil again. She had dark circles, ill-concealed by her makeup, under her eyes, and her shoulders slumped a little more than usual. He wanted to march across the courtroom and tell her to go to bed early today, but he shook off the urge. She wasn't his, and she couldn't be during this trial.

He'd be lying if he said he didn't wish it were different. He'd watched Sophia Anderson's lightning rise to the top with pride and interest since she entered law school. He had known how bright she was since she was eight, just as he knew she would be, and she was good at her job. Too bad. If she and Maria hadn't been so good, his team wouldn't have been forced to appeal the first two rulings. However, his client deserved a resolution in his favor, and Elijah refused to lose that for the man. The client and his family had been through enough. He needed to focus on that, not the overwhelming desire to drag Sophia into his bed to see if she was more than a temporary obsession borne from wanting what was forbidden.

Unfortunately, he couldn't get her off his mind, and he was desperate to deal with this increasingly uncomfortable attraction to the petite brunette with piercing gray-blue eyes. Every time she looked at him, he hardly managed to keep his focus on whatever he was meant to be doing. It had been torture trying to maintain his usual persona in the courtroom with her there, and he suspected Maria knew it, though she had the good grace not to mention it. Sophia seemed the only one out of the three of them who *didn't* know the power she held, which only made her that much more appealing.

This most recent appeal should be over in a month or two, and it would be the last any of them made.

I could have her then, he reminded himself. He was legendary for his patience and persistence. So why did two or three months seem like an eternity? In all his 34 years, Elijah had never been this way with women, but with her, he was. That was the most worrying thing about this.

He settled into his seat beside his associate and tugged at the collar of his dress shirt.

"Everything all right, boss?"

"Fine. Just a little warm in here today."

The associate cast him a dubious glance and then returned to his work with a shrug. Elijah rubbed his temples and tried not to look at Sophia. He had to make it through two more months. Just two more. He was merely infatuated with Sophia, not in love, and he could wait that long to quench his thirst—if she proved amenable. He hoped that for once, she'd understand he didn't want to debate the merits of his wish to act on this urge and would give in. He'd watched her over the last two years, and he was confident he wasn't the only one interested, however oblivious she was to his own interest. Yes, two more months. Two more, and he could have her.

***

Waiting another two months proved impossible. Elijah found he lacked the necessary self-control for the first time in his life. He shouldn't be doing what he was doing, but he'd called Sophia up to request her for documents she'd been asked for earlier in the week. She was supposed to send them up by courier in a week, but he'd made up some excuse to get her to bring them up herself. He waited impatiently for her to take the elevator or the stairs from her firm's offices two floors down to make her way to his office.

The two of them could face serious consequences for what he was about to do if she agreed to it. Even if they weren't disbarred, the whole trial might have to be retried, which would cost everyone dearly. That was why no one was going to find out.

There was a knock at his office door.

"Come in."

The door opened, and Sophia stepped in with a frown on her face, clutching a folder with the files his team had requested from theirs. She shut the door behind her and shuffled in, dropping the folder onto his desk. "Elijah."

"Sophia," he murmured, eyeing her wrist where the bracelet he'd gifted her for passing the bar always rested. "Thank you for bringing them."

"Your excuse was one of the dumbest I've ever heard." She crossed her arms. "What did you really want, Elijah?"

He cleared his throat and smiled tightly. "You always did see straight through any of my nonsense. You want it straight?"

"Have I ever wanted anything else?" She sat in the chair across from him and crossed her legs. "*Summoning* me up here like this is going to raise questions."

"No, it's not. You can just say I demanded urgent delivery of the files, and you didn't have a courier, so you brought them yourself. You're not the junior partner in this case. People would probably believe it."

"Fine." She recrossed her arms. "Spill, then. Why did you really call me up here?"

She wanted it blunt and unequivocal, as usual. For once, he wanted to dance around it. What he was about to say was crossing a line he couldn't uncross. "Soph...what I'm about to say might sound somewhat indelicate, but you'll give me a chance, won't you?"

She raised a brow. "Elijah Clarkson, are *you* tongue-tied? This is a first!"

"I want you," he blurted out, hating that there was no better way to say this now that he'd started. "And I'm sick of waiting for the trial to end to say it."

Her eyes widened, and she stiffened, barely breathing. "W-what?"

He groaned and rounded the desk, grabbing the arms of her chair and leaning close. "I can't put this much more bluntly, Soph. I want to sleep with you. You're like a drug I can't get off my mind. I want it too badly to keep waiting. Two years of waiting is enough."

She gasped, cheeks coloring. "Elijah! You...you can't possibly be serious."

"I am." He eyed her with a frown. "I didn't misread you, did I? You want me to, don't you?"

She didn't speak. He waited, heart hammering in his chest. She did, didn't she? She had to. He'd known her since childhood. He couldn't have mistaken the signs.

"Sophia?" he prompted softly. "Please tell me this wasn't a horrible mistake...I...I made one back when I got involved with Maria, and I'd never forgive myself if—"

"Elijah, we can't."

"Because you don't want to?"

She flushed and looked away, but she didn't say yes. "It isn't right. We could end up disbarred if anyone finds out."

"No one will. I promise. Besides, Soph...I'm asking you for a few nights."

Her blush deepened. "Seriously? You're not only asking me to risk my license and career, but you're asking me to risk it for a few nights with you?"

"What would it take to convince you?"

She looked away, hurt flashing on her face. "Elijah, I...I don't know if I can do this."

"Then let me help you decide..." He could tell she wanted him, but she needed a push to give in.

He leaned the last few inches to caress her mouth with his. She whimpered, but she didn't push him away, and her hands went to the lapels of his suit coat. That was all the proof he needed, but he wanted to hear her acknowledge what she wanted aloud. She tried to pull him closer.

Elijah smiled against her mouth and then pulled away just enough that she couldn't easily recapture his lips with hers. "Do you want me or not?"

"I..." The red in her cheeks crept to her ears as she tipped her face up to his. "I sh-shouldn't."

"I don't care about shouldn't, Sophia. Obviously, I don't, or I wouldn't have kissed you or asked you any of this. I think that kiss proves you want me, but I want to hear you say it. Do you want me or not?"

"I do," she whispered softly.

"Then say yes. Come see me at my place. It's a gated community. My staff can pick you up; no one will ever know."

She shifted in her seat, staring down at her lap. "You don't know what you're asking of me."

"Are you afraid you won't enjoy it? I promise our secret will be safe, Soph. You can count on it."

She looked near tears. "I'm afraid you won't give anything more. You're asking me to settle for being your toy."

He flinched. "That's not how I meant it. If you didn't want me, I'd apologize and beg you to forget I ever brought it up. I'd spend an eternity trying to make it up to you. But you do want me, and I want you."

She laughed sadly. "I've always wanted to hear you tell me that. Only you could find a way to make it the last thing I'd hoped to hear."

"Soph..."

"Fine," she whispered. "Is that the only way I can have any part of what I want?"

"I..." He sighed. For now, it was, and he wouldn't lie to her about that. "Yes."

"I guess I'll take what I can get. But Elijah? I'm not going to settle for warming your bed forever. If that's all you'll ever give me, don't expect me to stay."

He didn't. He just needed to burn her out of his system. Once he did that, they'd go their separate ways. But the pain in her expression tugged at something deep inside and made him wish he could promise more, wish that he hadn't been so badly burned with Maria. His girl-next-door deserved more. If he were a better man, he'd give it to her, but he wasn't going to lie to her about who he was now. He'd never lied to her, whatever other pain he'd inflicted at times. "I don't expect you to. Frankly, I think this is a matter of wanting the forbidden for both of us. We'll deal with it and move forward before one of us does something foolish."

She stood with a sharp nod. "Very well. Maybe you're right."

Maybe? He was. He'd never been wrong about these things. Except with Maria...he'd been wrong with her. Could he be wrong here? He opened his mouth to ask her something, but she turned and walked out, leaving him to contemplate her parting statement.

Maybe you're right. With Sophia, that always meant, *but you're probably not.* He sighed and shifted in his chair. This time, he would prove her wrong. He was right about this. He had to be because to have anything more meant risking too much. Their careers, their licenses, their hearts. That wasn't a risk he was prepared to take.

Chapter 2

Sophia stepped out of the car and strode to the steps of Elijah's enormous mansion on the outskirts of Chicago. She'd never seen a private estate this big. He'd purchased the land surrounding it and had turned it into a fair imitation of an old Victorian estate in England with the sort of privacy he'd promised he could offer. At least he hadn't lied about anything, even if he had ripped a little piece of her heart out in the office earlier that day.

She'd hoped to hear Elijah Clarkson tell her he had wanted her since her late teenage years, and now, when he finally said the words, they'd come in all the wrong ways.

Part of her still screamed. This was lunacy. Agreeing to this cheapened her to nothing more than a thoroughly desired lay he'd cast aside in the end. She knew agreeing would only bring devastation in the end, that they'd never regain their friendship after crossing this line.

Still, she'd said yes because a bigger part of her hoped that she'd read her old friend correctly, that he was lying to himself by claiming he only wanted to burn her out of his system. Perhaps in time, he might change his stance and offer her his heart, not just his body. That was the real reason she was here, ringing the bell and listening to the tinny sound echoing inside the enormous mansion. The door opened, cutting off any reverie. Elijah stood on the other side, a warm smile on his face.

"You came."

"I said I would."

His smile fell, and he stepped aside, drawing her inside with him. "Sophia, listen...I know how I asked wasn't very delicate––"

"It could've been worse." She smirked, trying to cover the raw pain the reminder brought with sarcasm.

He sighed and scrubbed a hand over his face. "I'd first ask you out on a date or two if we could do that, but we can't. I couldn't wait anymore, Sophia. I hate seeing you on the other side of the courtroom and knowing I can't show you just how easily you snap my self-control."

She laughed and shook her head. "Elijah, you've demonstrated perfectly how easily I apparently snap that already. Where is the bedroom?"

He grimaced. "We don't have to go straight to—"

"You didn't want anything other than sex, Elijah Clarkson. Renegotiate the terms of engagement if you don't like them."

"I suppose I deserve that," he murmured. "Fine." He pulled her into him and pressed his lips to hers in a teasing kiss. "Is this better?"

She shivered. Even though she hated how they'd ended up here, she couldn't deny that she wanted him or that she loved even that brief touch of his mouth on hers. "Maybe a bit, but you can do better."

"Hmmm." He smiled slightly and trailed his lips from her mouth to her jaw and down her neck. "How is that?"

Her skin tingled everywhere he touched, and she moaned gently. Even his teasing touch was enough to fog her mind, though she retained a deep-seated sense of hurt and pain at the knowledge that there might never be more than sex between them. "I still think it could be better," she whispered.

"Better?" He shook his head. "Hard to please much, woman? Very well. What do I need to do to redeem myself?"

She smiled sadly at the familiar bantering between them. Why couldn't he see that she loved him, that she wasn't Maria and didn't want anyone else? Didn't want anything more than she wanted Elijah Clarkson to take charge and love her. She wanted this, but she knew it wouldn't be enough on its own.

She needed more, needed to know he saw her in his future as more than a fun lay or merely a friend.

Now wasn't the time to focus on that, though. In time, he might open up and come to see her as more than a desire he could burn out of his system.

For now, she wanted him to soothe both the ache of need he'd created and the pain of longing he'd ignored.

"There are too many clothes in the way for my liking." She played with the buttons of her blouse. "You want to redeem yourself, Elijah? Perhaps we can move this to the bedroom?"

He scooped her up with a smile. "Demanding little thing, aren't you?"

"Demanding and little, maybe. A thing? Most certainly not," she replied gravely. "You need to stop thinking I'm a thing you can use and toss away."

"I meant the remark kindly," he muttered, heading for the bedroom. "Don't take it the wrong way. Are you still pouting over how I asked you over here? If you want to argue over methods, I'll oblige. I'd much rather strip you and kiss you senseless before I take you, but I'm not insensitive. We can talk first."

She turned her face away. Once he started kissing her in earnest, she'd lose herself in the need she also felt for him. She wouldn't want to talk anymore. She didn't want to talk now, either, though. She'd agreed to take what she could get, even if it should be degrading to even consider agreeing to such a proposal. "No. We agreed. Sex only. Nothing permanent. I don't want to talk."

"We always used to talk to each other before this. I'd like to think we're still friends."

"You can't cross the Rubicon and pretend everything's the same on the other side, Elijah. Either we're friends, or you're sleeping with me for a fun fling."

"You mean more to me than that, Soph," he whispered, hurt flashing in his gaze. "I'd never..."

"You don't like to imagine that's what you're doing, and maybe I do mean more to you than that, but you certainly aren't proving it with your actions."

He set her on the bed in his master bedroom and stepped back as if she'd bitten him. "Don't be unfair. You agreed."

"Yes, I did." She reached back and unbuttoned her skirt, shimmying out of it before starting on the buttons of her blouse. "Well? Are you going to help?"

He chewed on his lower lip, watching her with a mixture of lust and uncertainty. "I think maybe we should talk."

"There's nothing else to talk about. You want me. I want you. There's nothing more to it. Your words, Elijah. Not mine."

"Fine." He stalked over and stood between her thighs, pressing them further apart. "But don't say I didn't try to be a gentleman."

"I'm under no delusion that you are a gentleman. A gentleman wouldn't have asked me what you did."

He reached out and grasped her chin in his long fingers. "One last chance, then, love. Do you want me, or don't you?"

She smacked his hand away with a bitter smile. "Don't you dare call me that. As for wanting you, I may hate myself for the rest of my life for it, but yes. I want you, Elijah Clarkson. Now for God's sake, stop slapping me in the face with it. Make me forget that desire has made me stoop so low or so help me God. I will walk out right now."

He smiled sadly and cupped her cheek. "If that's what you want."

As he stripped her out of her blouse to expose the lacy black bra she'd worn for him, she closed her eyes and wished desperately that were true.

If her wish were his command, she'd have more than this stolen moment with him.

His lips trailed a line of fire from her jaw down, and she surrendered to the sensations, letting his touch wash away the pain his refusal to give more than this left deep inside.

Later she would let herself hurt over it, knowing full well she'd go back if it meant having just one more taste of Elijah. She wanted him too much to say no. If she was his drug, he was her kryptonite.

Chapter 3

When she next faced Elijah, it was in the courtroom. She watched him enter, but he didn't acknowledge her, and she sank back in her chair, ripping her gaze away from him. Of course, he wouldn't give her the time of day in public. She was his dirty little secret, and he'd never be seen treating her as a lover in public, even if he wanted her as such. He'd made it clear. He didn't have room in his heart to love her like she wanted to be loved, and any hope for it was foolishness.

"Are you all right, Soph?" Maria eyed her with concern.

"I'm fine," she whispered, watching people filter in as the jury took their seats.

"You don't seem it. If you need to step out, I can handle the case today."

She straightened, pulling her jacket taut and buttoning it. "No. I'm fine. I just...I blew off some steam with some guy last night, and it didn't go like I'd hoped."

Maria's brows rose. "Straightlaced Sophia Anderson and fling do not go in the same sentence. What happened?"

"I'm not a fling sort of girl." Her cheeks burned in shame because that wasn't entirely true; for Elijah, she was. What did that say about her? "And that's precisely why it didn't go as I'd hoped."

Maria made a sympathetic sound of understanding. "He didn't tell you he didn't want more?"

"No, he did." She slumped in her seat. "I agreed anyway, and now I'm kicking myself."

"Girl, you have it bad for this guy if you agreed to sleep with him knowing he wouldn't give you the commitment you wanted. Either that, or you were drunk. Were you?"

She gaped at the older woman, who had become a friend as well as a role model in the last few years. "No! Jeez, Maria. What do you think I'm doing at night? I don't go out drinking when I have to prepare for court the next day."

Maria shrugged. "Just asking...so it's the first. Who is this guy?"

She forced herself not to look at Elijah, even though she could sense he was staring at her. "No one, you know...anyway, I didn't have a chance to tell you yesterday, but Mr. Clarkson has those files he'd asked about. I had to take them up. The man-made some stupid excuse to have me running documents like a courier." She rolled her eyes. "He thinks too highly of himself."

Maria snorted. "Sometimes, but Elijah probably just did it to see you."

"What?" Her heart hammered in her chest. Could Maria suspect? "No, I don't think so...I think you're imagining things. Mr. Clarkson wouldn't be interested in me. I'm sure I'm not his type."

"Right. Sophia Anderson, you can't possibly be that naïve! The man's had his eye on you for the last two years. I'm surprised he hasn't made a move yet. He has more self-control than he did with me. In fact, it's impressive, considering that he's been pining after you for as long as I've known him. It was always Sophia that and Sophia this when we were together. It grated after a while."

She knew...

Sophia swallowed hard, wondering why Maria hadn't said anything all this time.

If she had known Elijah and I had had a past, why did she ask me to be on this case? Sophia mulled.

"We were...he and I were childhood friends, Mar, and I was his

19

paralegal while I was studying for the bar. He probably just talked because he was proud of me and still feels some of that older brother sort of affection he had for me when we were kids. He's probably not interested." She sneaked a peek at him and found him watching her discreetly too. "It would be highly unprofessional for him to make a move, even if you're right. He knows better."

Maria pursed her lips. "Maybe, but he's not known for always playing by the rules."

"You can't seriously be accusing him of breaking rules and cheating!" She was momentarily distracted from trying to throw Maria off this train of reasoning. "He wouldn't."

"No, but he's not afraid to exploit loopholes or engage in risky behavior. He hasn't had any complaints from clients or other lawyers. He's good at doing things quietly when he needs to." Maria frowned at her ex. "But I know him well enough to know he's interested in you, Soph. Maybe it's that he's not sure you're interested, but if he asks while we're on trial, I'll rip his head off. This is your first major trial, and if he messes it up for you, I'll personally make sure he's the one disbarred."

Sophia shrank down in her seat. "That's...that's probably not necessary, Maria."

"It is absolutely necessary. Costing you your license on accusations of collusion is unacceptable. He might or might not lose his license normally for it, though he'd be in trouble. If he tries, I want you to tell me." Maria stood as the judge entered the room.

Sophia followed suit. It was a little late for that. He'd already asked, and she'd already agreed. There was no way she'd ever tell Maria that. She wouldn't risk getting Elijah in trouble, especially when he'd promised her he'd keep *her* from getting caught. However she felt about their arrangement, and however angry she was with him for his methods and refusal to offer her more, she'd never go that far. He was a good lawyer and didn't deserve to lose his license for being a blind fool when it came to her.

***

Elijah caught up with Sophia and Maria in the parking lot. He wanted to pull her aside and speak to her privately, but the expression on Maria was thunder. He didn't know what he'd done to tick her off now, but he wasn't going to give her a good reason for being angry by conversing with Sophia privately and giving the appearance they were friendly with each other.

Not when they were so close to the end of this miserable trial.

Besides, he was only indulging himself with Sophia to rid himself of this pesky desire so they could go back to the way things were meant to be as friends.

The thought rang hollow even to him as he stared at the woman he'd had writhing underneath him the previous evening. He already wanted her in that position again, staring up at him with those vulnerable, wide eyes.

This time, though, he wanted her without the tears that had come last night as they lay in bed together. She'd been quiet, and he suspected she thought he'd gone to sleep, but he hadn't. He'd listened to her sniffling for a while until she was asleep, and he lay awake long after, questioning everything he'd done.

He should've understood this would hurt her that day in his office when she'd told him she'd take what she could get. It had been such an obvious remark, such an obvious hint that she had liked him for some time.

He'd brushed it aside because he hadn't *wanted* to think that as much as she wanted sex with him——it would destroy her to give up her body in addition to her heart without any chance at having his in return.

"What do you want, Clarkson?" Maria asked in a clipped tone. "If you're here to congratulate Sophia again like you did two years ago and again at the end of the last appeal, you can get lost. You're going to start rumors if you keep this up. Lawyers from opposite teams don't congratulate one another on wins that cost them and their clients. You're no different except with Sofia."

A warning note echoed in her last remark, and he bowed his head in acknowledgment. "I needed to speak to Sofia, Maria. I promise I'll be brief and discreet."

Sofia gasped. "Mr. Clarkson, I—"

He shot her a warning look.

"What do you need to discuss with her?"

"Does it matter?" Elijah stepped past Maria toward Sophia.

His ex stepped into his way with a scowl. "Elijah, so help me...you're not pulling this secretive bull you always did when we were an item. What do you want from Miss Anderson?"

He fixed her with a glare of his own. "Nothing that pertains to the trial."

"Not good enough." She crossed her arms. "Well?"

"Fine," he growled, knowing she wouldn't move without a good reason.

Maria wouldn't tell anyone about their prior friendship, given how long ago it had been, and there was no reason not to use that information to spin a small lie to get her off his back.

"*Miss* Anderson and I are old friends, if you have to know, and she was my paralegal while she studied for the bar, which you well know. We've been professional about the situation to avoid a conflict of interests, but it's been two long years of working in that courtroom with a friend and keeping my distance. Can't you give me five minutes? I have something private I need to talk to her about, and it has nothing to do with the trial. I wouldn't ask if it weren't important, Maria."

Her eyes narrowed. "Five minutes, then, Clarkson."

He didn't need to be told twice. Grabbing Sophia's arm, he tugged her away from her boss and toward the corner of the building where they could talk without appearing too cozy. At least if he had her there, and they spoke quietly, it would seem like he'd caught up with her to ask for something related to the case. It was believable enough.

Sophia followed along without a word, glancing at the empty parking lot. The hearing today stretched past the normal dinner hour, and few people were still around. He could practically hear her worrying about this publicity and what people would think. He stopped on the steps off to the side in Maria's line of sight. "Stop worrying about what people will think. Look at me."

She did, but she couldn't seem to hold his gaze for very long.

"You were crying last night."

"You must've been dreaming." She laughed and looked away. "What we did...it was fun. Why on earth would I be crying after that?"

He scowled. "Sophia Anderson, I have never once lied to you. I expect the same courtesy."

Her cheeks heated, and her hands balled into fists at her sides. "Stop this, Elijah...we're in public, and I don't want a scene."

"Then just admit you were crying and tell me why."

She glanced at Maria and then met his gaze, eyes glassy with unshed tears. "If you don't know, Elijah, then you're a fool. Think for five seconds, and maybe you'll figure it out. When you do, maybe you'll know why you should apologize."

"Come to dinner over the weekend," he murmured. "We can talk about it then."

"Why should I?"

"I'm trying, Soph." He didn't want to say he already knew why she was upset and wanted the privacy to make her admit it, to try to make this right. He also didn't want to admit that one night with her hadn't been even close to enough. So much for burning her out of his system.

"You didn't want anything more than what we had last night," she murmured. "Dinner isn't part of that."

"It could be. We could renegotiate terms."

A spark of hope lit in her expression before she tamped it down and looked away, hiding her feelings from him as best she could. "You don't negotiate. You decide and expect everyone else to agree, just like you had yesterday when we first spoke about this. How is that now different?"

Because he'd realized how much of a fool he really had been to think she could keep emotions out of this. He wanted her so badly but didn't want to ruin her. If she told him she couldn't handle it without getting entangled with him so badly that she'd break when he'd finally managed to burn this desire for her out, he would back off and deal with it on his own. He cared too much about the woman in front of him to push her to do something she didn't want or couldn't bear.

"It's different because you're...I care about you. You're a good friend, and we need to talk. I messed up yesterday, maybe more than once, and I'm not taking no for an answer on this, Soph. Come to dinner."

She sighed and looked at Maria, who was tapping her wristwatch with a frown. Then her gaze returned to him, and she nodded. "Fine. Dinner over the weekend. Goodbye, Mr. Clarkson."

He shoved his hands in his pockets to keep himself from reaching out to her and watched her walk down the stairs to rejoin Maria. She murmured something to the other woman that seemed to satisfy Maria's curiosity and then strode to her car.

He stood and watched until she was out of the parking lot before walking to his own car with a low curse.

What was he doing?

He'd said nothing more than sex. Now here he was, asking her to come over for dinner and trying to renegotiate something that would offer her what she needed. He didn't *have* what she needed, though, and it wasn't a good sign that he hated the idea of walking away.

Groaning, he climbed into his Ferrari. He could be an unfeeling jerk at times in this business. That's who he had to be on the outside. It wasn't who he was inside, or at least, he hadn't thought so.

Now, when Sophia really needed him to walk away from her because he wouldn't give her his heart—which was what she desperately wanted and needed—he couldn't find that legendary self-control of his long enough to let her go.

This was insanity and couldn't end well, but here they were.

Sighing, he took off, heading for home. There was too much he needed to sort through, and it didn't feel like there was enough time for it.

Chapter 4

Sophia stepped into the entry hall of the mansion, staring up at the chandelier she'd failed to notice last time she'd been here. Elijah had a habit of distracting her, even from things she should face, and didn't wish to––like the reasons she'd cried herself to sleep next to him a few days ago after he'd taken her the first time. He'd made the physical intimacy memorable and almost sweet at times, but by the end, that had only been salt in an open wound. It reminded her that she would never have his love and heart. Only his lust.

She turned her focus to the paintings on the walls. He had a Rembrandt on display in the entryway.

Just how much money did Elijah have?

She trailed along, looking at each painting in turn. The names on these were only slightly less recognizable than Rembrandt. A piece, these cost more than she made in a whole year. Being one of only two senior partners at a firm paid a killing, it seemed.

"You like them?" Elijah's low timbre filled the entryway, bouncing on the marble floor and wood-paneled walls.

"You display wealth like a peacock struts about displaying feathers," she muttered. "How much was the Rembrandt?"

He shrugged. "I don't remember. Dinner awaits. Shall we?"

She stared back at him. He waited, hands in his pockets, as if he wanted her to come to him. Tensing, she considered walking back out. Having this dinner was a slap in the face after his proposal that they have no-strings-attached sex. As if sleeping with Elijah could *ever* be no-strings-attached to her.

"Come, Soph," he murmured. "We agreed."

She stiffened. "I know what we agreed. But maybe we should just have the conversation now and skip dinner."

He gave her a long-suffering look. "Really, Sophia. I'm not a patient man, but I'm trying."

For you, the tone seemed to imply. Could he really be trying to temper his usual intensity for her, to talk to her like he'd once done when they were young?

"Why?" she whispered.

"Because I care."

About her? Or just about making certain she was willing to continue warming his bed? She straightened further and walked to him, heels clicking on the polished stone. "Fine. I can endure dinner."

He put a hand on her shoulder. "Endure? I'd hoped you might enjoy it."

"Have you given any thought at all to what I said on Thursday?" she asked coldly.

"A great deal. That's why I asked you for dinner. I want time to discuss things without the temptation to ignore our chat in favor of my bed." He tipped her chin up. "Wanting to burn you out of my system doesn't mean I don't care. I just..." He exhaled softly.

"You just what?"

"I don't want to feel like this."

"Like what?"

He released her with a groan, scraping his fingers through his hair. "God only knows...for once, I'm not sure what to do, Sophia."

She cracked a smile and tried to lighten the mood. "I can tell you what you *shouldn't* do."

He eyed her with a shake of his head. "I don't doubt it. Look, Soph...I don't want to *want* a woman I've known since she was a little girl. I can't get you off my mind, and I'd hoped sex would help."

"Did it?" She crossed her arms. "Are you content now?"

"No. It made it worse."

"What a shock," she remarked flatly. "But I thought you wanted to eat."

"I do, but you're angry now, not just hurt. Tell me what I've done. Tell me how to fix this."

"You can't."

He flinched.

"You can't because you don't want to risk what it would take to fix it. Now I'm hungry. Let's finish this discussion over dinner," she added.

He looked away and headed down the hall. They walked in silence until they reached a door at the end of the hall. He opened it to reveal a warmly lit dining room with candles on the table, flames dancing merrily, and soup bowls full of piping hot soup set across from each other. "Dinner, then?"

She let him guide her inside and seat her, her gaze fixed on the candles. Why had he lit these? What was the point? It added a romantic flair that she doubted he'd intended.

"Don't you like them?" Elijah took his own seat across from her and fiddled with his napkin. "I lit them for you."

"Romance hardly fits into our situation."

"Sophia..."

"Look, you wanted to know what was wrong. How to fix this?"

"Desperately."

"Do you love me? Is that what has you scared about your interest in me?"

He blanched and stared down at his soup. "I don't know. Once, I thought I loved Maria, but I was wrong, and she didn't love me like I'd thought. The relationship was a nightmare, even if I let her go amicably."

"What makes you think she and I are even vaguely similar?"

"I'm the same person. What if I'm wrong again?" He lifted his gaze to hers. "I don't think I could let you go like I let her go, Sophia. I already don't want to let you go now, even if I know I should. Even knowing you can't keep feelings out of it and that it may break you, I still want to hold on."

She looked away, pondering both the words and her response. If he couldn't let her go like he'd let Maria go, that meant he felt more strongly about her than he did Maria or others he'd been with. "Are you normally this possessive?"

He barked out a laugh. "Not usually, no. Maria will have told you about the string of women after her."

"You've set your sights on me, but I'm different than the rest."

"Yes, God help you..." His voice sounded strangled.

When she glanced up, she found a mixture of shame and frustration in his gaze. "You'll do anything to have me, even if you know having your bed and not your heart will break me? Really, Elijah?"

He didn't answer, and he dropped his gaze away from hers.

"You're crueler than I remember." She pushed away the untouched soup, appetite gone. "Why, Elijah?"

"I don't know." His voice tightened. "I don't understand why I...Soph, I don't want to hurt you, but I need to know why I feel this way."

"Maybe you're lying to us both tonight," she suggested softly.

He stared at her like she was a lifeline, even as he claimed he needed nothing but her body. Even this dinner said there was more to his feelings than mere lust. He wanted something, but he was afraid to name it, and his fear would be the end of them both at this rate.

"I'm not like her, Elijah," she whispered. "But if you keep pushing me away and holding me at arms' length, you will break me, and I will either walk away or become a shell of my former self trying to be the elusive ideal you crave."

"I don't want some elusive ideal," he murmured back. "I want you. I just don't know if I want you like *that*. How can I know? It could be mere infatuation, the longing for the forbidden."

She rose and set aside her napkin. "Well, let me know when you've decided. I'm too tired to warm your bed tonight. I'll see myself out."

"Soph..." He stood and reached out for her before letting his hand drop back to his side.

"Figure out what you want before it ruins us both. No more of this if you only want me in your bed. I can't bear it," she whispered hoarsely.

"I'm sorry."

"I know. Just not sorry enough to let me go if you don't want me here permanently." She smiled sadly. "I hope you know what you're doing."

"I don't," he admitted. "I don't, Soph, and it terrifies me."

"You know where to find me if you want me. Call. Text. Email. Just do me a favor. Don't ask me over again until you figure out how to untangle it all." Turning her back on him, she walked out, her heart breaking with each step.

Deep down, she knew she'd return to his bed if he wanted her, and that terrified her more than anything. How much of her would be left when Elijah was through with her? What if she was making a terrible bet in believing that, given time, he would realize he wanted her permanently? What if she'd misread his conflicted, pained replies tonight, and he wasn't struggling to recognize love? It would break her, but she couldn't let go of the hope. Not yet. Not even if it would wreck her in the end.

Chapter 5

Elijah spent nearly four weeks thinking about what Sophia had said. He'd struggled to keep his distance and fought with himself over calling her, but he'd forced himself to respect her wishes. Once he knew what he wanted, he'd call.

Four weeks of pure torture later, and he knew for a fact that he'd done both of them a massive disservice by failing to consider his own emotions more closely. He was terrible with personal relationships for all his success in business. He'd never regretted that more than he did now, but hoped that Sophia wouldn't hold it against him.

The trouble now was that he didn't know how to tell her things had changed. He didn't want to come out directly and just say he was in love, but how should he go about it otherwise? Maybe it was best he simply admitted it in as blunt a fashion as he'd suggested he take her to bed. He entered the courtroom and caught her gaze across the divide between the two teams. They were presenting closing arguments in another two weeks, and things were dragging on too long. He was ready to be done with this, and the look on her face said she was too.

Guilt warred with the relief that he could now proceed, knowing what he wanted. He'd put her through an emotional wringer, and she hadn't deserved that. It had been callous, cruel, and foolish to suggest they engage in no-strings sex to begin with. He owed her an apology, and he'd probably be apologizing for his stupidity for the rest of his life if she'd even have him. What if he gave her everything, as he'd done with Maria, and she fled? He'd already made such a mess of this. Maybe one more mistake would be the last straw. He stared down at his notepad with a frown.

"You all right, boss?" One of his firm's senior associates leaned over and handed him a coffee as he sat down. "You seem...tired."

"I'm fine," he murmured. "Thanks for bringing the coffee."

The door to the judge's chambers opened, and he rose along with everyone else, waiting until the judge sat to flop back into his seat. He'd been fighting for a dismissal of the previous ruling on the grounds of mistrial and failure to consider all of the evidence for a while. New information had come to light in the meantime, and now they were going over all of that too. The back and forth was becoming obnoxious.

"Wish the judge would just call it in favor of our client." Another senior associate settled into her seat with a groan. "It's obvious the defendant breached contract at this point, if it wasn't two years ago."

"It's just how these things go. Everything goes through a fine-toothed comb before a decision is made if we want to win this without another appeal." He rubbed his temples with a sigh. "But I know what you mean...hopefully, in a few weeks, it'll be the end of it."

"I hope so," she muttered, sipping her coffee.

That was the end of conversation as the judge called on them to present the last of the evidence. They'd adjourn court until the final arguments were made on the court date in two weeks. This was their last chance to lay out anything they had. Hours dragged by before they adjourned for lunch.

He cornered Sophia as they were leaving the courtroom and bent to murmur, "Dinner at my place tomorrow night at seven."

She looked up at him with a searching glance and then nodded. The crowd surged around them, and Maria pulled her away with a perfunctory glance at him. He let her go. They'd sort this out.

Now that he knew she was it for him, he'd do whatever was necessary to have her.

***

Sophia stepped into the mansion for the first time since their argument over the last dinner. Why had he invited her this time? He'd kept his distance for four agonizing weeks, leaving her to wonder what he was thinking and where they stood. Now he'd swept back in and ordered her over in that commanding, expectant tone of his. He'd commanded, and she'd obeyed.

Elijah stood waiting in the dining room when his butler showed her in. He held the back of her chair, candlelight dancing along the planes of his face and casting shadows over his skin. When she entered, he lifted his head to stare.

Something about the stare was different than usual. She couldn't put her finger on it exactly, but she knew it was different. There wasn't anything on the table yet, either. Just Elijah and the candles gleamed in the center of the table. She shifted, suddenly self-conscious, and pulled at the hem of her short black dress. "You asked me to come, so here I am," she murmured, the words sounding deafening in the room's stillness.

His gaze roamed over her before settling on her face. "Thank you. I thought we could take a walk before we eat."

"Where? You never want to be seen with me in public unless you think it can be excused as some professional interaction."

He frowned. "Doing otherwise would risk your career and mine."

"I'm aware." She pulled her sweater closer. "Where did you want to walk?"

"I thought we could walk in my aviary."

"Not outside then."

"No," he murmured, eyeing her as though he anticipated this was a trap. "Why?"

"You don't even want to be seen with me in the privacy of your own gardens." She frowned. "I know we can't risk the trial, but it's private on your property, and there are places well out of the city we could go. I'm not so hurting for money that I can't afford to go to some out-of-the-way town in the cornfields to spend a free weekend relaxing with you. You've never once suggested it."

His lips pressed together, and he looked away. "It didn't occur to me."

"Why is that?" She crossed her arms, shivering. "Are you ashamed of me?"

He frowned. "This isn't how I wanted dinner to go, Soph. I brought you here to tell you something important."

"You've decided then?" If he had, should she read into his behavior right now?

He stepped over to meet her and cupped her cheek in his hand. "I have, but I...I'm not ready to say it yet. I wanted to show you the house, though."

She smiled softly. He wanted to let her in. The house was merely a gateway into his life. It was his way of saying he was willing to take a risk, even if he wasn't yet ready to name the emotions he felt toward her. "I need to know what you want this to be soon."

He stroked her cheek and bent his head to capture her mouth with his. His lips caressed hers gently at first and then more urgently, as if he were trying to convey everything he couldn't say in that single kiss. When he finally released her, she was breathless and staring up at him in surprise. He'd never kissed her like that before. The behavior was confusing. Elijah wasn't one to hide from what he wanted once he knew, so if he knew how he felt about her, why didn't he want to say? Was it that he felt guilty for what he'd done to her?

"I know. What I want isn't what we had. I am so sorry for how I handled this at the start, Sophia. I never should've treated you like that." Guilt flashed in his eyes, and he dropped his gaze from hers, stepping back. "I want to make it up to you, make it right somehow."

She wrapped her arms around her torso, any happiness at the step forward dimming. "Is all of this because you feel guilty for what happened? I don't want a relationship based on lies or on guilt."

His head jerked up. "No! It is absolutely not because I feel guilty. How could you even think that's what this is about?"

"Can you blame me after how you convinced me to come to your bed, Elijah?" She stared at him, hurt, warring with confusion, and then anger. "You start by telling me you're ready to give us a chance, the one thing you know I want, and in the next breath, you're apologizing for what you've done and pleading for forgiveness. It seems like all of it is geared toward not losing me."

"It's not about keeping you!" He raked his hands through his hair. "I mean, not keeping you in my bed...I want to keep you *with* me. I want the chance to learn to love again. Maybe you're the one I can do that with." His voice softened. "Maybe this time I can give everything and not lose the one I loved."

"Then prove it's about more, Elijah," she whispered back. "You want to have a fresh start? I'm willing to give it, if you can show me you aren't trying to hide me away. Let's go do normal couple stuff. Far away from here to minimize risks, but if you aren't trying to hide or make things better to ease your guilt, it shouldn't be a hard request to honor."

He bit his lip and stared at her. Finally, he nodded. "We'll go somewhere for the weekend. Pack a bag and tell Maria you're taking a short trip to see family further instate. I'm taking you to dinner at one of my favorite childhood places."

Chapter 6

Sophia hurried to the private runway, wondering where they were going. She'd met Elijah after he'd moved into her neighborhood here in Illinois near the Chicago suburbs, but she knew only that he'd moved from neighboring Indiana to come here when his father had taken a surgeon's position in Chicago. His father had since moved back to retire out here, but Elijah had remained in Chicago for his law practice.

He didn't speak much about his childhood, perhaps because his mother had walked out on them when he was young, and his father had struggled to care for a young teen while working in a demanding hospital environment. Even after he'd moved in next door in his teens, her mother often took him into their home when his father couldn't make it home until the early morning hours. He'd practically grown up treating her mother as his.

The downside to that was that she had no idea what to expect. Elijah had asked her to pack warm clothes for the fall weather, so she assumed they'd be outside some of the weekend. Butterflies rioted in her stomach. This was straight out of her childhood and teen dreams featuring Elijah and a romantic getaway, but she was afraid to let herself hope he might be coming to see her that way. Or that he was doing this because he genuinely meant it when he said he wasn't trying to hide her and wasn't ashamed of their relationship––or whatever was going on between them.

She walked to the hangar door and found him lounging inside

by the steps into the plane. He pushed away from the side of the jet and strolled to meet her, his long legs eating up the distance and his hair uncharacteristically tousled. A smile curled his lips, softening the harsh planes of his face.

"Here. Let me take the bag." He didn't wait for her to protest, taking it from her and lifting it easily.

"Thank you," she murmured. "You're certain the staff here won't say anything or leak this to the press?"

"I'm certain, Soph." He stopped and cupped her cheek, leaning down to kiss her gently. "Stop worrying."

She released a soft sigh and leaned into him for a moment. This was really happening. Elijah was letting her see something from the childhood he never spoke about, the years before her. That was big, especially for Elijah, who was used to keeping even the smallest things private from most. He was letting her in, just as she'd wanted. It left a warmth deep in her chest that spread to everything else.

He kissed the top of her head. "Come then. We're ready to take off."

At his wave toward the cockpit, the plane roared to life. She hurried to follow after Elijah, clambering up the steps onto the plane. He stowed her luggage and led her to the back, where there was a small door into a private compartment. "It's going to be about an hour long flight. I told the pilot to take the...scenic route." He offered her a roguish grin. "I thought we could take advantage of the private quarters."

She stared at the giant round bed in the center of the room and flushed. "Won't the owner of the plane mind?"

He laughed. "He doesn't."

"You know him that well?" She turned to find him grinning.

"Sweetheart, *I* own the jet."

Her breath hitched, and she spun in a slow circle, taking in the gleaming chrome, and oak surfaces and the small windows with shades pulled over them. "You own *this*?"

He walked over to the bed and sat down, patting the space at his side. "Is it really that hard to believe?"

"I...I don't know." She joined him and laid back on the bed, staring up at the white plastic ceiling. "I just never imagined you were rich enough to own a jet."

"I don't flaunt my wealth." He dropped back to lay beside her. "Now...about availing ourselves of the facilities..."

The plane shuddered and began pulling out of the hangar. He sat up and pulled her over to the seats near the window, buckling her in. Then he buckled himself in beside her with a smile. "What do you think?"

She glanced at the door with a frown. "Are the doors soundproof?"

"No, but the flight attendant knows not to disturb me unless I call him with the intercom. He'll stay up at the front of the jet. He's not going to hear anything." He placed a hand on her thigh. "If you don't want to, we won't. We can curl up and watch a movie instead."

She bit her lip with a smile. "I think this time you should work for it, Mr. Clarkson. Can't let you think I'm easy."

He grimaced. "Sophia Anderson, I would never...no one who knows you would make such an error."

And yet he had with his ill-conceived, harebrained scheme to get her into his bed without letting her in. At some point, however, she had to let that go. It had been stupid, but he was here now, trying to make it right. It was clear he'd rethought his position, at least a little bit. "I expect dinner first when we land."

He nodded. "Movie it is, then."

They settled as the plane leveled in the air. Once it was steady, Elijah unbuckled them both and scooped her up, carrying her over to the bed. They spent the remainder of the flight nestled in pillows and blankets, her head on Elijah's chest and his fingers stroking her hair.

By the time they arrived at the airstrip near Elijah's childhood home, she was ready to eat. He guided her out of the plane, retrieving their luggage on the way out and laughing at her eagerness to disembark. She didn't care if he found it amusing. She was ready to see this part of his life, the one part he'd never allowed her into. "How far is it to the restaurant?"

He unlocked a Maserati and packed their luggage into the trunk with a shake of his head. "Not far."

"Why is it your favorite?"

He bundled her into the passenger's seat with a smile, but he didn't answer her until they were out of the airfield and on the road through cornfields and stretches of open country. "My mother used to bring me to the place I'm taking you when we went to pick my father up from the airport." His smile faded. "It's the last place she took me before she disappeared."

"Oh..." Her enthusiasm softened to sadness mingled with curiosity. She pushed aside her interest to think about how he might feel toward the place. "Elijah, we don't have to—"

He reached over and pressed a finger to her lips. "Hush. I chose the place, remember?"

"But it's...it's so personal."

"That's why it's perfect." He pulled off the road into a parking lot in front of a quaintly decorated diner with neon signs and climbed out.

She frowned when he rounded the car and opened her door. "What are you doing?"

"Taking you to dinner. You wanted me to, didn't you?"

"Here?"

"Is something wrong with here?" He tensed. "I told you it was a childhood favorite, so I figured you'd realize it wasn't anything fancy...if it's not—"

She leaned in and wrapped her arms around his neck to kiss him. "No. It's fine, Elijah. It wasn't what I expected. I've never seen you outside of ritzy restaurants, bars, and law offices in Chicago. It's a shock to be reminded that you were a normal kid once."

"Good. You had me worried for a minute." He kissed her back, relaxing into her touch.

She relished the warmth of his lips on hers, his mouth exploring hers eagerly. Then she pressed gently at his shoulders, breathing shallowly and rapidly when he obeyed her silent command and pulled away. "We should go in, or we'll never eat."

"As you wish, my lady." He offered her an arm, grinning like a child.

She laughed at the silly gesture. How long had it been since she and Elijah had been playful with one another like this? She'd forgotten he could be anything besides serious or seductive. Taking his arm, she let him guide her inside.

The interior was warm and inviting, though the people were mostly wearing beat-up jeans or overalls. Farmers, probably. It wasn't a place well-off lawyers went to eat, but that made it that much more special.

It was self-seated, so Elijah guided her to a booth in the back where they'd be hidden from view of the rest of the restaurant's patrons. He helped her into the curved bench and slid beside her, his hand going to her thigh in promise of what would come after they ate.

Soon, a middle-aged waitress drifted over to take their drink orders. She stopped when she saw Elijah. "Elijah? Is that you?"

He frowned in concentration and then smiled politely in recognition. "Mol?"

"One and the same. It's been ages! I've been following your case on the TV. Everyone talks about little Elijah Clarkson making it big. No one thought you'd go into law instead of medicine, but we sure are proud."

He cleared his throat and shifted, adjusting his tie. "Really?"

"Really! If you have a moment while you're up visiting your father, stop in again and say hi. I'd love to catch up." She flicked a glance over at Sophia with a polite smile. "You look familiar.

Have I seen you somewhere?"

Sophia shifted to slouch in the seat and stared at the table. In jeans and a t-shirt, she probably didn't look much like Sophia Anderson, associate lawyer for defense council, but it still left her unsettled that this woman had recognized Elijah so quickly and had watched the case on TV. What if she recognized her and took it to the press? They'd be in so much trouble. "I just have that sort of face, I guess," she mumbled.

Elijah took her hand with a tight smile at the waitress. "Mol, we're in a bit of a rush tonight. My father is on a cruise, and he asked that we get to the rental in time to make sure the cleaner had the check he left for her. I'd love to stay and chat, but I can't. After we get back to his place, I have meetings. I can leave the city, but no matter how far I run, the clients don't stop demanding attention."

She laughed and flipped her ponytail off her shoulder. "Guess you're in high demand. I'll get the drinks. You ready to order?"

"Two double cheeseburgers, everything on them, and fries to go with. Thanks, Mol."

The waitress wrote it all down and left with a backward glance at Sophia.

Sophia groaned. "You took me somewhere everyone recognizes you?"

"Not everyone. I didn't think anyone in the diner would, Soph. We'll be fine once we get to my father's bungalow for the weekend. He said to make ourselves at home, but there won't be the usual maid service to disturb us."

"Good," she murmured. "I don't want the vacation ruined by a media firestorm."

He took her hand in his and brushed his lips across her knuckles. "That's not going to happen."

"I certainly hope not," she said, pulling her hand back with a sigh.

Deep down, though, Mol's obvious interest in the two of them left her worried. What if the woman told someone they'd been here? She didn't like the way Mol had stared at Elijah either. Too much keen attention, and her dismissive attitude toward Sophia nagged at her. She could've *tried* to be as friendly to Sophia as she was to her...

She hesitated and glanced over at Elijah to find him watching her closely. Her what? Boyfriend? Friend with benefits? Enemy in court and lover at night?

"You're overthinking, Soph. Just enjoy dinner."

She nodded and focused on trying to absorb everything about the little diner instead. This was her first and closest look at Elijah's childhood. He was right. She needed to enjoy the experience and have the amount of trust it took for him to show her all of this.

***

The weekend flew by in a blur. They were back on the jet to Chicago in no time, and she watched the Indiana landscape fall away from the plane window with a sigh. Once they were able to leave the seats, she curled up on the bed beside Elijah. He didn't ask her if she wanted to make use of the bed this time. Instead, he just spooned her and laid gentle kisses down the side of her neck and her exposed shoulders where the sweater had slid off to reveal her skin. He didn't try to take it any further, and she relished the warm, comforting moment with him. Soon, they would have to return to the façade they'd been maintaining for the last month and a half or so.

When the quiet announcement that they could turn on WIFI came over the speaker, she reached for her phone. She should check on her notifications to see what was going on. Maria might have tried to contact her since she knew Sophia was returning today. Others could've messaged about personal or work things too.

Elijah groaned behind her and tangled his fingers in her hair, pulling gently to grab her attention. "That can wait, love."

"It's been waiting all weekend, Elijah." She shifted to face him, pressing her hips against him and throwing a leg over his hip. "I just want to check it quickly."

He ground his hips against hers in a distracting rhythm. "I can make it worthwhile to wait a little longer."

She rolled her eyes and logged onto the internet with the plane's WIFI signal. "Stop it. It'll only be a minute."

His hands drifted to her hips and then to her butt, kneading and pinching gently. "Come on, Soph. Don't spend the little time we have left like this on checking emails."

She was about to answer when the notifications started pouring in, along with one notifying her of a new report on the trial. She'd set up alerts about those for the major news outlets. Nothing should've been happening while she was gone, though, so she wasn't sure what it could be. She clicked on the notification to read more.

INNOCENT OR GUILTY? POSSIBLE COLLUSION BETWEEN LAWYERS ON HANSON CASE TAKES EVERYONE BY SURPRISE.

Her entire body went cold, and she froze when the photo in the main article loaded. It was a bit grainy, but it was clearly a photo of her with Elijah in the little family diner they'd visited. The phone slipped from her hands and fell face down on the bed. "Oh, God, please, no..."

Elijah stopped teasing and sat up. "What's wrong?"

Her lower lip trembled, tears filling her eyes. "You promised this wouldn't happen!"

"What?" Confusion flashed across his face, and he picked up her phone. Then understanding mixed with fury shifted his expression. "How did they get their hands on this?"

"I don't know, Elijah. Ask Mol, maybe," she spat. Elijah

dropped the phone back onto the bed with a scowl. "Let me off on the runway. I'll walk back. I'm not going to be seen with you. It'll wreck my career and everything we've worked on these last two years."

He stiffened, his face going hard and blank. "I will not. It's not safe."

"I'll be fine."

"You have luggage."

"Keep it," she snapped. "You've done enough damage. I think I can bear the loss of my luggage to save my career."

"It's one story. No one has any proof."

"They have photos of us cozied up to each other looking like a couple." She stared out the window as the fury rose higher. "I'd say that's enough for everyone to believe them, even if the teams we're on don't."

"I'll fix it, Soph." His expression turned to pained pleading. "Please, get off at the hangar."

"No."

"The pilot can't stop on the airstrip. It's not allowed."

"Then let me off and wait to leave so we won't be seen together."

"No one will talk."

"People already have." She jammed her phone into her purse and stalked to the door. "I'll spend the rest of the trip in the main cabin. I don't want you anywhere near me, Elijah. Not until this is over. Maybe not ever if this goes really badly. I..." The tears pressed in then threatened to make an appearance.

He stood, starting toward her.

She shook her head. "Don't. Don't you dare. This is all your fault. You couldn't wait. You just *had* to proposition me, even after you knew I didn't know how to say no to the man I've wanted since I was in my late teens. You knew what could happen, and you did it anyway."

He scowled. "You insisted I take you out in public, Sophia! I didn't suggest that. If you hadn't—"

"I was a fool. A fool to believe we could work. A fool to say yes in the first place. A fool to ask for the fairytale I obviously can't have. But at least I wasn't the jerk who could justify asking the unthinkable and risking a friend's career."

"Soph..."

She raised a hand and turned, jerking the door open. "I don't want to hear it, Elijah. This is over until the end of the trial, and maybe forever."

He didn't try to stop her this time, and she slammed the door behind her before collapsing into one of the long, leather seats of the main cabin, the tears finally making their presence known. She curled into herself and cried, wishing someone would hold her and tell her it would be okay, but the only man who could do that was Elijah, and she couldn't bear to have him near her after what had happened.

That headline was the last straw; in this state, she simply couldn't handle looking at him, let alone having his hands on her. Her heart felt like it was breaking in two, and she didn't know if it would ever get better. If this cost her her license, she was going to be devastated. She should've known not to cave to Elijah's request. Now she was paying for her stupidity.

Chapter 7

Sophia hurried toward the front door of her building to go over final preparations for the trial with Maria. What had started out as one headline a week ago had morphed into a firestorm of media attention. She'd spent most nights seeing the trainwreck unfold in front of her. The worst part of all of this was the pain of being alone and missing Elijah's steady presence. Up until they'd parted ways when he went to college, he'd been her steady place. He'd listened to countless silly problems and given his support and friendship to draw her through them to a point where she too could see they had been silly, however big they'd seemed then. Now she didn't even have that, and she'd pushed him away for the sake of professional appearances.

A lot of good that had done. There were whispers in her office now too, and she suspected the rumors were flying on the two floors above that housed Clarkson and Holden Law. She didn't know how much longer she could handle this. She might as well take her relationship with Elijah public at this point; no one was arguing she hadn't been involved with him after seeing those photos. The only thing they were arguing about was whether any collusion had happened along with the incredibly unprofessional emotional entanglement. When the verdict came out on that, she might well lose her reputation, worse yet, her license.

A crowd of reporters in plain clothes lingered on the side of her office building, waiting for her or Elijah. They mobbed around her at first, shoving mics in her face and asking questions. She pushed her way through them before the tears and breakdown she felt coming on could make an appearance on national news. Before she lost it, though, the reporters pulled back and changed focus.

She turned to find Elijah standing there, hands in his pockets, looking sad—though to the reporters, he likely looked thunderous. She could see a hint of anger at their treatment of her boiling in the look he leveled on them. It said more about how he felt about her than any words ever could have. When his eyes met hers, though, she ducked her head and scurried inside. There were many people around to risk a grateful smile or even a nod. It would only give more weight to the rumor mill the press was running.

Her chest squeezed with a combination of emotional pain and panic. She'd been so foolish to think she could come out of this the same or even in one piece. It quickly became obvious to her that she needed Elijah, even if she couldn't have him. If she hadn't, she never would've agreed to his demeaning first request, let alone forgiven him for it. She made it to the bathroom and into a stall before she broke down in tears.

The whole affair was one humiliation after another, and she'd done it to herself. If she hadn't insisted Elijah prove he didn't want to hide her away, this never would have happened. She'd caused this problem. She'd been so stupid to think this could have a happy ending. Actually, she'd been foolish for going along with it all even though she knew it couldn't. She let herself hope it could end well when Elijah had invited her to dinner the second time, but she should have known better than that.

She tried her best to remain quiet as she cried to avoid adding further humiliation by letting everyone in the office know it was getting to her, but she must not have been very successful because, after a minute or two, she heard a knock on the stall door.

"Sophia?"

Maria. Wonderful. Could the tiled floor just open up and swallow me whole?

She straightened, wiping at the tears and clearing her throat a bit, hoping she didn't sound like she'd been crying for the last five minutes. "Sorry. I'll be out in a minute. I know I'm running late."

"I'm not upset about you running late. I'm concerned about your change in demeanor and the fact that one of the other girls came to tell me they heard you crying in the bathroom. Can you come out here, please?"

Great. Maria would probably lay into her for ever getting involved with Elijah once she knew the truth. She'd be furious at Sophia for endangering her license and risking the entire trial just to get into bed with a man who hadn't even been willing to admit his feelings to her and had chosen to deflect by making her his toy instead of a lover. She couldn't put it off, though, so she stood and straightened her clothes before opening the door to the stall.

"Come on. We'll talk in my office." Maria handed her a tissue. "Your mascara ran, by the way. Why don't you clean up a bit before we walk over?"

She nodded, her voice failing her, and went to the sink to blow her nose and wipe away the streaked mascara on her cheeks. Waterproof would've been her best option today. She'd thought about it and decided it wasn't needed. Another bad decision to add to the string of them she was making lately. When she'd cleaned away most of the traces of her tears, she turned to Maria. "I know I messed up," she whispered.

"We'll discuss it in my office." Maria took her arm gently and led her out of the bathroom through the halls.

The other employees were kind enough not to stare, though some stole little glances at the two of them as they passed. She flushed and stared at the ground. Could this get much worse? By the time this was over, she might be too embarrassed to even set foot in this building, assuming she had a license to practice when this was done.

Maria pushed open her office door and guided Sophia inside, closing the door behind them and locking it. "Why don't you sit down? You look like you're ready to collapse." She took a seat in one of the spare chairs and gestured to the one beside hers. "I'm worried about you, Sophia. I've seen the headlines, but I assumed they weren't true. That maybe you'd taken that photo with Elijah before the trial, and someone was trying to sabotage our last appeals. But you seem too upset for that to be the case. What's going on?"

Sophia dropped into the offered chair and buried her head in her hands, the tears threatening to make another appearance. "I've screwed up so badly, Maria." A sob hitched in her throat. "I'll be disbarred for sure."

"The collusion charges are true then?" Maria sounded horrified.

"No! No, they're not. But..." She looked up at Maria and sighed, "...I did get involved with Elijah..."

Understanding replaced the confusion and despair on Maria's face. "I knew it. I knew it was you he had his eye on. Honestly, I think the man was in love with you back when we were dating, which might be why he never seemed really happy."

"You don't understand!" Sophia wailed. "I know you think he was in love with me then, but he wanted it to be only sex, and now the papers are dragging our names through the mud because I slept with him."

"Please tell me you had the good sense to demand more than a one-night stand from the man." Maria looked aghast at that rather than the issue of the media. "He's not good at admitting his feelings, and if you let him, he'll just try to burn you out of his system. When it doesn't work, he'll panic and make stupid decisions."

"Sounds like it's something you know firsthand," she muttered. "Well, that's how it started, at least...It...I agreed to it, and it was more like any night he wanted than it was a one-night stand...I think it's more now, but he never had the chance to tell me. I was so stupid. I insisted he take me out in public to prove he wasn't ashamed of being with me or trying to hide me away like a dirty little secret."

Maria smothered a laugh. "Really, Soph? Why didn't you just ask him about it instead of insisting he prove it?"

"I guess I just wanted hard evidence." The tears slipped past her lashes. "Then, when I saw the headlines, I was angry and hurt. He'd promised this wouldn't happen, and here we are anyway. I can't be seen with him or be near him. It'll destroy my career and the trial."

Maria stopped laughing and reached out to take her hands. "Soph, we walk a tough line as lawyers, and often, we don't find a good work-life balance. You have a man who understands exactly how hard that balance is, understands exactly how hard you have to fight for your place in this sort of world, and he respects that."

Sophia stared at their hands in her lap.

"That's worth a lot. Elijah drives me crazy in the give-me-five-minutes-with-him-and-a-brick kind of way. But I see how he is with you, and it's not even close to how he was with me. He's protected you in this as much as he can by keeping the reporters at bay."

That much was true.

"The man's brilliant in a courtroom, but put him into interpersonal situations, and he's a bull in a china shop, but he'd do anything to make this right. I know both of you, remember? I've never seen him so miserable, not even after I ended things with him."

Sophia looked up at her boss and mentor with a frown. "You mean that?"

"I do. Knowing Elijah, he's either scheming or wracking his brain for the solution to win you back. Leave this in his hands, Sophia. He'll find a way to make it work if he wants you. When he does, give him the chance to make it right. I can see your love for him in the pained, longing way you look at him whenever you cross paths now. No job is worth losing that kind of love."

She stared at Maria with wide eyes. Had the woman who hated Elijah Clarkson's guts *really* told her to give him a chance, to risk her career if necessary, to take a shot at what Elijah was offering her? What was it that Elijah was offering, though? Until she knew that, she couldn't promise she *could* give him a chance. He might not be worth risking her job for rather than the other way around.

"Promise me you'll give him a chance and, by extension, yourself a shot at happiness." Maria squeezed her hands and let go. "You may not get another opportunity if you walk away from this one now."

Sophia swallowed back tears. "I'm scared."

"I know, but for all his flaws, when Elijah loves someone, he's the safest place to land, Soph. He will not drop you, but you have to trust him. He doesn't do well with people who fight him for control, but when someone hands it over, he would sacrifice even his life to make sure that trust is honored. I'm guessing that, unlike me, deep down, all you want is to trust him and let go."

Her cheeks warmed. "I'm a competent professional. I don't need to let anyone take care of things."

"Need and want aren't always the same. It's not a shame to be a pugnacious lawyer in the courtroom then go home to submit to a man who cherishes you. Don't let fear or pride get in the way."

She sucked in a deep breath. "Can I really submit to him and still keep a professional image?"

"I don't know. You might have to work for a firm that's not connected to him or what happened here, but I will gladly help you find that position if it's necessary. Knowing Elijah, he'll find a way to make sure it isn't. Just trust him, Soph."

"Okay." She peeked up at Maria from beneath tear-soaked lashes. "You're really not angry at me?"

"No, I'm not. Whatever they want to say about collusion, Sophia, there's no way you could successfully collude with him without my help since everything passes through me. Anyone who knows this trial knows I'd rather be raked over hot coals than collude or cooperate unnecessarily with Elijah." She smiled. "At least my reputation for hating him is useful for something."

"Thank you, Maria," she whispered.

"What are friends for?"

"I expected you to yell at me for my indiscretions."

"I'm not the yelling sort." Maria stood. "Well, shall we go over the final details and put this issue out of our minds for now?"

Sophia nodded, relieved to change topics. She filed Maria's advice away for later, though. The older woman had made some excellent points, and though she was still scared of committing if Elijah did find a way to fix this, she didn't want to let go of him, either. Maybe Maria was right. Maybe she could take a leap of faith and find a safe place to land in Elijah's arms.

Chapter 8

Elijah chased off the news anchors mobbing around him the moment Sophia had fled. With her safely inside, he didn't need to hold their focus any longer, and he hadn't decided how to handle this yet. Until he did, he wouldn't say anything to these people. Once he'd decided how to proceed, he could determine if a press conference would be of any use.

For now, he had a meeting with his partner. The two of them had to discuss the narrative the media was spinning and figure out how to handle it. He strode into the building and took the elevator to his floor. Stepping off, he walked through the quiet office space and past meeting rooms filled with lawyers working together on other cases his firm had taken on. He stopped at the end of the hall where his office and his partner's stood side by side and knocked on his partner's door.

Liam Holden opened the door with a grim look. "You always have been good at stirring up hornets, Eli."

"Good to see you too, Liam."

"Don't even start." Liam stood aside and ushered him in. "What were you thinking, man?"

"That I've been slowly going mad over the last two years watching her in that courtroom. Things got out of hand. I need to find a way to fix this."

"Fix it?" Liam whistled and shook his head. "Has it occurred to you the best way to 'fix it' might be to distance yourself from her?"

"Not an acceptable solution."

The word distance niggled at him, however. He needed a way out of this, distance from the problem. But he didn't need or want distance from his woman. That wasn't an acceptable route to take.

"I know that look." Liam groaned. "What are you thinking about now?"

Elijah pursed his lips. "Liam, I need a solution that doesn't involve letting go of Sophia."

"She avoids you like the plague now, I've noticed. Haven't seen her come up to deliver anything in weeks. Not since you returned from your trip to Indiana. Let me guess...that's where the picture was taken."

"Yes." Elijah hated laying out personal details like this, but Liam was his partner. Liam would have to take over if this went belly up on him.

Liam would have to *take over*. It hit him like a thunderclap. "Wait...I think I might have an idea. Liam, I know this is a bit unusual, but what if you took over the case?"

"What?" Liam pushed back from his desk and shook his head. "But you're handling it. You know more about the situation and the files."

"I'll help you behind the scenes. You'll have all my notes, all my case files, everything. But if I remove myself from the case and do a press conference to explain I want to pursue Sophia without the accusations of collusion or concerns about the conflict of interest, we could solve this whole mess."

Liam settled in his chair with a frown. "I don't know, Eli. It's a big risk. If you admit that you were involved with her previously, you're risking *confirming* in the minds of the public that there was something untoward happening."

"There's zero evidence of it."

"Not yet, but you know there could be a mistrial claim filed over these accusations if Maria decides to pursue it."

"She won't."

"She hates you," his partner pointed out.

"But not enough to stoop to that level. She won't believe the press. Even if she believed I could cross that line, she *knows* Soph wouldn't."

"Soph, is it?" Liam shook his head. "You have it bad, Elijah."

"I've 'had it bad' for a long time," he admitted. "But that's not the issue right now."

"Does she know?"

"Liam, I value you a great deal as a partner, but you know I don't do personal chats."

"What I know is that it's Clarkson and Holden Law Services we have on our sign, not just Holden Law. What you do affects the business just as much as mine does. My name's not the only one connected to the prestige this company enjoys, and this whole personal matter has become very public, risking our careers and our firm." Liam crossed his arms with a raised brow. "So I'll ask again. Does she know, Elijah? Does she know you're in love with her, and is it worth trying to fix this?"

Elijah shifted in his seat, hating that he felt like a bug under a microscope. His personal life was his own, and he didn't want to lay it bare before anyone, not even a man he'd come to consider a friend. Liam was right, though. It had become personal. "No, she doesn't know. I didn't have a chance to tell her."

"One would think you'd *open* with that, Elijah," Liam drawled.

"Well, I didn't," he snapped. "Can we just leave it and focus on a solution?"

"Not yet." Liam's eyes narrowed. "Why are you so defensive about this? Why *didn't* you open with that?"

Elijah looked away, ears burning. "Fine. I don't want to talk about it because I bungled it all up at the beginning and then managed to bungle it even worse by taking her someplace people knew me when I'd promised her it was safe. I thought it was, but I was wrong, and now she's hurting because of me. *Again.*"

"Again?" Liam looked aghast. "What in the world did you do in such a short time that could cause pain worse than what she's going through with this media debacle?"

"I proposed we have no-strings-attached sex so I could burn her out of my system even though I knew she was infatuated with me and would say yes to anything that gave her some small scrap of my attention," he admitted with a sigh. "Yes, I know. I was an idiot."

"I had another word in mind," Liam remarked coldly. "What would possess you to do such a thing?"

"Not thinking clearly. I...look, it's no secret Maria's leaving messed me up badly. I didn't want to risk anything. I was going to tell Sophia I'd come to my senses and was in love with her when she misunderstood my reasons for apologizing and demanded I prove I wasn't hiding her away in shame."

"So you took her to dinner back in Indiana and spent the weekend there with her?" Liam groaned and rubbed his temples. "And your solution to this is that I take over the trial so you can try to patch things over?"

"A rather oversimplified way of putting it, but yes...I need to fix this; I can't do it if I stay on the case. By the time the case is over, assuming it even ends on time in a week, I'll have lost her. I can't do that, Liam. I'm asking as both your friend and your partner...help me out on this."

"Fine. But you'd better make things right with that poor woman. You've hurt her enough, Elijah. Don't make it worse." Liam pointed a finger at him. "Hold a presser tomorrow and fix this. Then go sort things out with your woman."

Elijah rose with a nod, relief coursing through him. "Thank you, Liam. I'll owe you one."

"Yes, you will. Now go figure out what you're going to say. That interview will probably make national news." Liam waved him out.

Elijah left, wondering if he was going too far and if Sophia would let him fall without catching him. For once in his life, he depended on someone else to catch *him,* and he was terrified she wouldn't. Despite the fear and uncertainty, though, he had to do this. He had to try to make things right by her. Honor and love demanded it. His need for her demanded it. It didn't matter if she was there to catch him in the end or not. He'd never forgive himself if he didn't try.

***

Elijah sat under the bright studio lights with the news anchor from the station he'd contacted. They'd been the first to break the story about him and Sophia, so it seemed only fitting that they'd put this misunderstanding to bed with his interview and announcement.

The camera light blinked to green, a steady pulse marking the passage of time much like every rapid beat of his heart. He looked to the news anchor with a raised brow as if to say, *Well, get on with it.*

The anchor, a middle-aged man who was balding and red-faced as though he were perpetually angry, straightened in his chair and leaned forward with an engaging smile at the camera. "Folks, we have Elijah Clarkson live in the study with us. You heard that right. Live in the studio. The man who has been avoiding the press like the plague has finally come out of hiding and offered us an exclusive interview."

Elijah smiled begrudgingly at the camera when the man behind it gave him a wave, the cue to look at the camera and look pleasant. They'd been over the details before he'd taken his seat up here behind the long frosted surface of the table.

His host turned to him. "Well, Elijah, we're delighted to have you here today."

He just bet they were. What news agency wouldn't be given the recent manufactured scandal? "I'm honored to be here."

"So tell us...when you contacted the studio, you said you

wanted a chance to air the truth about you and Miss Sophia Anderson. So what is the truth, Elijah?"

"The truth is that we were not involved during the trial. I hate to disappoint viewers, but we weren't colluding or even romantically involved."

"But the photos—"

Elijah held up a finger. "Ah, yes. The photos...an old friend's claim to fame gone wrong, sadly. I took Sophia home to Indiana for a weekend to ask her if she would consider a relationship with me. You see, I've known her since we were both younger, and I've wanted her for a long time. This trial, as everyone knows, has dragged on for an interminable amount of time, and I've grown tired of waiting."

"So what did she say?" The news anchor leaned forward in his seat as though hanging on Elijah's every word.

A cheap trick for the audience. What he was saying might fly in the face of the media's wild speculations, but it wasn't all that riveting. "I never had an answer from her on my question," he admitted quietly. "Your story jumped the gun, broke a story that misunderstood our involvement, and scared her off."

The news anchor made a sympathetic sound. "That's a tough break, my friend. Are you going to try again?"

"Yes, but not before I ensure the collusion issue is out of the way. We've both worked too hard on our respective teams to have the case declared a mistrial on speculation." He smiled tepidly to show there were no hard feelings about it, though that was a lie. He'd like to strangle whoever had messed everything up between him and Sophia with that ill-conceived article. "I'm going to hand my case over to my senior partner, Liam Holden, so that I can pursue Sophia without endangering the integrity of the trial."

"You must really love her to do something like that. This is a big case and a big client for you."

He stared down at his hands. The first time she heard him say those words shouldn't be on TV in some scripted interview. The anchor was going off script, and he didn't have to answer. "That's between me and Sophia. I came here to clear both of our names by speaking up about what was really going on. That's all."

The anchor took the hint and smiled broadly at the camera. "Well, that's all for today, everyone. We'll see you back at the top of the hour for the weather report."

The camera light blinked red, announcing the end of the broadcast, and Elijah rose, hurrying down the steps. The anchor tried to stop him, but he had somewhere to be and someone to apologize to. He just hoped what he'd done up there on stage would be enough to convince her he meant business and wasn't playing around anymore.

Chapter 9

There was a knock at her door around nine the evening before the final hearing. Sophia frowned and rose. Who would call at this hour? She glided to the front door and opened it to find Elijah standing on her doorstep in a t-shirt and jeans, looking more casual than she'd seen him in a long time. Dressed like this, it was as if he'd shed his usual persona of Elijah Clarkson, business lawyer extraordinaire, for her Elijah, the one she'd known as a child and loved as much as a naïve little girl could. "Elijah?"

"Soph. Can I come in?"

She hesitated, glancing back at the messy apartment and noticing the lingering scent of Chinese takeout. The place wasn't suitable for visitors.

"I won't be long if you don't want me here, but I need to talk to you." He stepped closer, his chest brushing hers. "Let me inside."

This time it was a command with a hint of underlying uncertainty. She didn't like seeing him unsure. He was always so confident, so in control. To see him vulnerable at all left her unsettled. She stepped aside and let him in, closing the door behind him. She remained facing the door, hand on the doorknob as she wrestled with the emotions that seeing him always brought up. A new one flooded over the old ones, though. Hope. She'd seen his interview and knew he was serious about fixing this. But she was terrified that if she trusted him now, he would break her to pieces.

"Soph," he whispered behind her. "Look at me, please."

Tears filled her eyes, and she shook her head and then lowered it to hide behind a curtain of her wavy hair. His hands settled on her shoulders, turning her gently. Then she was enveloped in his embrace. He smelled of his usual cologne––fresh pine, and earthy cedar tickled her nose.

He scooped her up and carried her to the sofa. When he sat down and cuddled her close, laying down so that she could lay on his chest, she knew he had no intention of hiding from his own feelings or hers anymore. He stroked her hair gently, whispering soothing nothings until the tears subsided. After the tears had gone, she lay in silence for a long while and listened to his steady heartbeat, letting the rhythm lull her back to a steady calm.

"I came to apologize for how I started this whole mess," he murmured. "I never should have done that. I never should have lied about my feelings or what I wanted."

"No, you shouldn't have," she agreed.

He tugged at her hair just enough to make it sting. "Brat. I'm groveling here, and I never do that. Let me do it in peace, would you?"

She lifted herself to stare down at him, straddling his hips to sit more comfortably. "You shouldn't have. I'm not going to disagree and argue you did nothing wrong."

He soothed her with a nod of agreement. "All right. I'm sorry for everything I did, Sophia. I'm sorry for how I hurt you and for being the dumbest man alive about this stuff. I'm sorry, but I'm hoping you'll let me make it right."

"Didn't you do that when you gave the trial to Mr. Holden?"

"That wasn't enough. I want you, Sophia. I love you."

She tensed. He couldn't have said what she thought he had. Earlier, while watching his interview, the anchor had implied as much and tried subtly encouraging Elijah to say it on air, but he'd refused, claiming it was private. Had he really just told her the anchor was right? "What?"

"I love you," he murmured. "I love you even if you won't forgive me and give me a second chance, but I'm pleading with you to do both, Soph."

Calm replaced the tension. She was afraid, but Maria's warning came back to her before she opened her mouth to tell him she wasn't sure. If she didn't trust Elijah, she would never have what she wanted. He was a safe place to land, but she had to trust him enough to jump first. "I want to try, but I'm scared...Promise me you'll catch me if I fall? That I can...That I can..."

"Trust me?" he whispered.

She nodded.

He leaned up and kissed her softly. "Always and forever, from now on."

"Okay. I'll give you a second chance, but if you mess this one up..."

He kissed her more thoroughly. "I won't, but I never want you against me in the courtroom again, Soph. It wouldn't work out well. Come work for me instead, so we never have a case between us again."

She straightened and shook her head. "No. I need to make my own way, Elijah. We'll just have to work things out because I won't have people thinking I grew my career by doing my boss. I'm sorry..."

He sighed. "I figured that would be the answer. Very well...we'll find a way to make it work. Together, Soph. I promise it'll work out."

She smiled down at him. "I'm going to hold you to that."

***

Sophia dropped her keys into the bowl at Elijah's front door and kicked off her shoes. She shook her head at the Van Gogh painting he'd recently mounted with a sigh. The man really did spend ridiculous amounts of money on art.

Elijah ambled out of his den and down the hall toward her, a welcoming smile on his lips. "How did it go, Soph?"

"You don't know?" Thinking about it brought a rush of frustration. "I thought you'd watch it live."

"I wanted to hear it from you." He wrapped her up in his arms and kissed her forehead. "But based on the look on your face, I'm guessing it didn't go well."

"No, it did not. I lost. We lost"

"I'm sorry."

"Really? Your former client won."

"Well, I'm not sorry he won," Elijah amended. "He was the wronged party. But I'm sorry you lost your first big case."

She sighed and rested her cheek against his chest. "I hate losing."

"I know. But Soph? You've just had your first and most important lesson since you passed the bar."

"I have? It feels more like a punishment than anything..."

"Certainly not." He tangled his fingers in her hair and tugged her head up so he could see her face. "Don't ever think that about losing a case. It happens. But in this case, you lost fair and square because your client was guilty. Sometimes, Sophia, it is all right to lose the case so that justice can be served. You have a duty to give your client the best defense you can, but when there is no defense for their actions, and the evidence shows it, don't ever feel guilty for losing."

She bit her lower lip. "That's not what we're taught in law school."

He kissed her mouth gently. "I know. Consider it rule number one from Elijah Clarkson's school of law."

She laughed and shook her head. "All right then. Dinner?"

"Absolutely. I'm famished. If you want to rant, you can tell me more about the case while we eat."

"No, I think I'm all right. I don't want to think about the case tonight."

"Good. I have other things we can discuss and other things we can do."

She rolled her eyes and headed for the dining room. "I'm sure you do, Elijah. I'm sure you do."

Epilogue

A year later

Sophia couldn't wait to share her news with Elijah. She was a bundle of nerves and excitement, and she hoped he'd share in that excitement once she told him. Insecurity mingled with her joy, dimming her enthusiasm.

What if he wasn't happy?

What if he didn't want this as much as she did?

It would bring a great deal of change into their lives, and he might be unhappy about that.

Elijah strode in, carrying the gourmet takeout and caramel apples she'd asked for. He took one look at her face and placed the takeout on the counter to rush to her side.

Cupping her face in his hands, he looked her over, trying to decide what had caused the distress.

"Are you all right, love?"

"I think so."

"Good. You look a bit pale, though. Why don't you sit down on one of the stools while I plate the food? I have something to ask you, and I don't want you fainting on me."

She fidgeted with her sweater and stared at her lap.

Elijah pinned her with a more stern look, crossing his arms. "All right. Out with it, Sophia. Why do you look nervous? Did you do something I should know about?"

"I..." Her ears warmed, "...well, it's more what *we* did than anything," she admitted.

"What we did?" He went from stern to confused. "I don't understand."

"Well, okay. Sort of part what we did and part what you did."

"I am not in the mood for riddles, love."

Well, there was no time like the present. "I'm pregnant."

The words were out in a rush and hung in the air, waiting for an acknowledgment from Elijah. He stood, staring at her in mute shock for a long moment. Then he blinked and shook his head.

"What?"

"I'm pregnant," she repeated.

She had to resist the urge to shy away in fear of his judgment. He didn't speak for a long moment, just staring down at her.

She stared up into his gaze as he processed her confession. Then a slow smile spread across his lips. "Really?"

"Really."

He bent and kissed her. "You really know how to one-up a man."

"One-up?" She frowned.

He dropped to one knee in front of her, pulling a small black box from his pocket.

Oh. She covered her mouth with one hand as he took the other and opened the box.

"The baby announcement has kind of stolen my thunder, but I guess I can forgive the kid," he teased. "Marry me, Sophia Anderson."

As usual, he wasn't requesting. He was demanding. But underneath the command, she heard the note of vulnerability, just as she had on the night when he'd come over to ask for a second chance, which she'd given despite her fears.

Now she was glad she had.

Tears filled her eyes, and she nodded. He slid the ring onto her finger with a broad smile and pulled her hand away from her mouth, leaning up to kiss her.

"You've made me a very happy man, Soph."

"And you've made me a very happy woman," she whispered. "Thank you for being a safe place to land, Elijah."

He kissed her more thoroughly and murmured against her lips, "Forever and always, love. Forever and always."

~ THE END ~

If you enjoyed *Lawyer Billionaire Daddy*, take a look at a sneak peek of the next book in the series: *Ex-Military Billionaire Daddy*.

Prologue

Maddie Hayes surveyed the lavish spread of food on the table. When Liam had asked her to come over for dinner with her three-year old son Trystam, he'd asked what she wanted to eat. She'd told him she missed the luxury of a good steak and potatoes, but she hadn't expected this. The cook had prepared fresh, made-from-scratch mashed potatoes, perfectly seared steak garnished with parsley and lemon, steamed vegetables, and crème brûlée for dessert.

"Is everything all right, Mad?" Liam's sister Jessica settled a moderate portion of steak and potatoes on her plate before passing the dish to Liam. "You're staring at your plate of food like you can't quite believe what you're seeing."

Maddie looked up from the plate, heat flushing her cheeks. "Oh...everything is fine. More than fine." She met Liam's attentive gaze and cleared her throat, shifting in her seat. "It's more than I imagined when Liam asked me what I wanted for dinner."

Jessica laughed. "You know my brother doesn't do things halfway, Maddie. Of course he'd make sure dinner was spectacular."

Liam smiled indulgently. "I had to do something special to convince you to come back. Good food seems to be the only way I can coax a visit from you these days, and with my busy schedule at the security firm, I can't exactly drop in whenever unannounced. I'm glad you could make it."

She smiled back and dropped her gaze to the plate of food in front of her. Liam had done so much for her. She couldn't quite believe he still wanted her around after all he'd seen her through. Trystam's father leaving for a job opportunity in another state while she was a few months pregnant had devastated her, made worse by him saying a child would only slow him down. But Liam—who had just returned from a long, difficult tour in Iraq—had stepped in to help as soon as he heard what had happened.

He'd been starting up the security firm in those days, barely a year into operating it, yet he'd often spare time from his schedule to look after her. He'd show up to check that she'd had lunch and taken her vitamins, staying over to keep an eye on her in the early days when she was sick often. And he'd taken her to the hospital when labor hit. He'd been there even though she'd wished the man who'd put her in this position was instead, and he hadn't once complained about her late-night rants or the emotions that followed as she struggled to move past her ex.

Liam had been furious with her, offering to drag her ex back and set him straight, but she'd refused to give him her ex's details, including his name.

Even after all that, he still made time for her and wanted to see her and Trystam. She glanced at the baby monitor on the sideboard across the room and cut into her steak.

"Don't worry about him, Maddie," Liam murmured. "You're here to take a break. He's sleeping in my room, and he's fine. He's getting big now, and he can handle getting up and calling for us if he needs you."

She nodded and released a slow breath before digging into her food with enthusiasm. She hadn't had a good meal like this in a long time, and she certainly hadn't been eating anything close to it in the last few months. She and Trystam had been surviving off macaroni and cheese, peanut butter, and toast. Sometimes she managed a little chicken, but things were tight right now, and she rarely had the money to afford it.

"So, how are things at the vet?" Jessica asked before taking a bite of her vegetables.

Maddie swallowed the bite she'd taken, her appetite ebbing. "Oh...they're...fine, I guess."

Liam's eyes narrowed, his usual response when she lied to him. He hated it when she kept secrets and told half-truths or outright lies. If she'd been his to care for, she expected he'd have taken her to task for it more openly and sternly, but the expression on his face perfectly conveyed his irritation and disappointment, anyway. "Maddie," he murmured in a warning tone. "Just fine?"

She shifted in her seat and swallowed hard. "All right...they closed a few months ago."

"Oh..." Jessica frowned. "Well, have you been able to pick up more hours at the diner?"

"I've tried. They don't have the hours for me."

Liam scowled. "So what have you been doing to pay bills and put food on the table, missy?"

"What is this? The Spanish Inquisition?"

"You'd know if it were an inquisition," Liam drawled. "Right now, I'm just asking."

Jessica stifled a smile. Maddie shot her a glare. So much for sisterly solidarity from her best friend.

"I'm waiting." Liam set down his silverware. "Maddie?"

Will Maddie finally admit that she needs help and is struggling to provide for her son? What happens when a blast from the past threatens the safety of her son?

Book 3 is available on Amazon now!